VIOLET INVESTIGATES

.•. The Hidden Treasure .•.

THIS BOOK BELONGS TO

....

HARRIET WHITEHORN

ILLUSTRATED BY BECKA MOOR

SIMON AND SCHUSTER

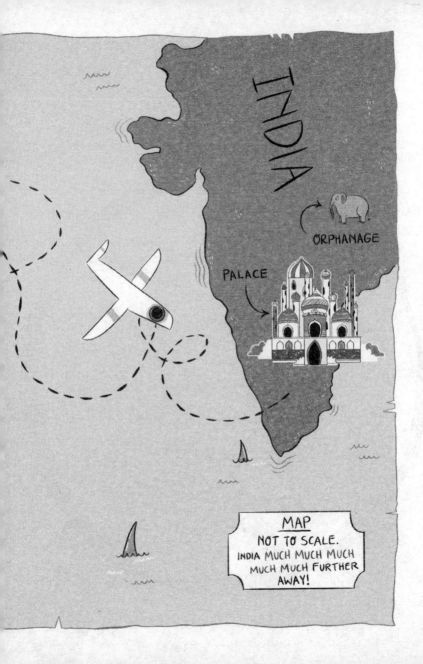

FOR POPPY – HW

FOR CALLUM – BM

First published in Great Britain in
2014 by Simon & Schuster UK Ltd
This edition published in 2022

Text copyright © 2014 Harriet Whitehorn
Illustrations copyright © 2014 Becka Moor

1 3 5 7 9 10 8 6 4 2

Simon & Schuster UK Ltd
1st Floor, 222 Gray's Inn Road
London
WC1X 8HB

www.simonandschuster.co.uk
www.simonandschuster.com.au
www.simonandschuster.co.in

Simon & Schuster Australia, Sydney
Simon & Schuster India, New Delhi

A CIP catalogue record for this book is available from the British Library.

PB ISBN 978-1-3985-1847-6
eBook ISBN 978-1-4711-1898-2
eAudio ISBN 978-1-4711-7647-0

Printed and bound by CPI Group (UK) Ltd, Croydon, CR0 4YY

MIX
Paper from
responsible sources
FSC® C171272

This is a story about Violet Remy-Robinson.

Violet lives with her mother, Camille, who is a jewellery designer, and her father, Benedict, who is an architect, and her cat, Pudding. When her parents are working she is looked after by a housekeeper called Norma. She also has a godmother, Celeste and a godfather, Johnny. You should know that Violet is a brilliant at two things – climbing trees and poker – both of which she is mostly forbidden from doing by her mother.

She lives in a flat that backs onto a large communal garden, which all the people who live in the houses around the garden share.

In the garden, there are lots of other children and they are divided into three  groups – the littilees who are under seven, the midders who are seven to eleven years old (Violet and most of her friends are midders) and the twelvers, who are older. Violet's special friends who live on the garden are Rose, her best friend with whom she also goes to school, and an eccentric lady called Dee Dee Derota.

Violet is always on the lookout for adventure and, a few months before this story begins, Violet and Rose solved the case of the Pearl of the Orient. A family called the Du Plicitouses had moved into the house above Dee Dee, bringing their cat, Chiang-Mai, and their butler, Ernest (who is now a great friend of Norma's), with them. A little while after they moved in, Dee Dee's valuable brooch was stolen and Violet – with a lot of help from Rose and a little help from a policeman called PC Green (very little, Violet would say, although PC Green may say differently) – solved the mystery of its disappearance.

I think that you can tell a good deal about someone by their favourite things, so to introduce you to all the people in this adventure, I thought I'd tell you about their most-loved possessions . . .

VIOLET

CAMILLE

Her grandmother's charm bracelet. Each charm is of a famous French landmark.

The 'Best Young Detective' award she received after solving the mystery of the Pearl of the Orient.

BENEDICT

GODFATHER JOHNNY

A scale rule that once belonged to a very famous architect called Le Corbusier.

His lucky pack of cards, which has never failed him yet.

ROSE

Red ballet shoes with ribbons that she was given for Christmas, but are a bit too special to actually wear.

ART

THE FOOTBALL THAT HIS FATHER GAVE HIM FOR WINNING A FOOTBALL MATCH.

ANGEL

AUTOGRAPH BOOK FULL OF FAMOUS SIGNATURES.

GODMOTHER CELESTE

DEE DEE DEROTA

HER PHOTO ALBUMS FROM HER HOLLYWOOD STARLET DAYS.

HER CAMERA.

PC GREEN

HIS POLICE CAR WHICH HE LIKES TO DRIVE REALLY FAST WITH THE SIREN ON – EVEN THOUGH HIS SERGEANT HAS TOLD HIM NOT TO.

RAJESH

A SPECIAL BOOK OF INDIAN POETRY GIVEN TO HIM BY THE MAHARAJAH, WHICH INCLUDES POEMS BY TAGORE, HIS FAVOURITE POET.

But I know you must be impatient for me to start the story, so come with me to a faraway place . . .

This story begins on New Year's Eve in a palace in India. Violet was busy helping herself to a large plate of chicken curry, rice, dhal, samosas and anything else she can cram onto it, from a long table groaning under the weight of umpteen dishes of deliciousness.

What on earth was Violet doing there? You may well ask. Well, let me tell you – Violet was at the end of a week's adventure in India with her godmother, Celeste. Violet had had the most marvellous time trekking through

the jungle, photographing tigers, and riding on elephants. She had spent her last few days of the holiday helping at a girls' orphanage run by a friend of Celeste's named Hari.

That afternoon, Violet had been teaching the girls how to play rounders when a pink Rolls Royce had pulled up in front of the orphanage. An elaborately dressed servant had stepped out of the car, with an invitation for Hari, Celeste and Violet to a New Year's Eve party at the Maharajah's palace that night.

'The Maharajah is the orphanage's benefactor,' Hari explained. 'He visits us often and the children love him. You will like him; he is an elderly man but has a young spirit, and he loves to meet new people.'

'What a treat for our last night!' Celeste exclaimed. 'Quick, Violet. We must run and pack our things, as we leave very early in the morning. And you had better wash the last of the jungle out of your hair and wear that beautiful dress your mother insisted you bring – how lucky we didn't use it to make a sling for that poor baby elephant like I suggested.'

The Maharajah's palace was made of pink stone and situated right in the middle of the city of Bochir. It was full of loud, chattering guests who reminded Violet of birds in their brightly coloured silk clothes. The air was thick with the smell of delicious food, making Violet's tummy rumble, so she left Celeste and Hari chatting with a group of people and made her way to the table of scrumptious food.

'I do so love food, don't you?' a voice said behind her, just as Violet was trying to ease a little more coconut curry on to her plate. She turned around to find an elderly gentleman in a very smart pink suit beaming at her.

'I used to adore jam roly-poly and custard when I was your age,' the elderly man continued. 'I was sent away to boarding school in England, which was a terrible experience I have to say, except for every Wednesday evening when we would have jam roly-poly and custard and I would be in heaven for a few minutes. And the Shakespeare – I loved that too. But apart from those two things, it was awful – cold showers, Latin verbs and other horrors.' He shivered slightly at the memory. 'But, I am being rude, I must introduce myself properly, I am the Maharajah of Bochir.'

Violet didn't know whether she was supposed to curtsy but she decided to give him a big grin instead, and that seemed just fine. She was about to introduce herself when a young man, wearing a splendid Indian outfit and carrying a pale pink cockatoo, walked over to them.

'This is my manservant, Rajesh,' the Maharajah said. Rajesh bowed deeply to Violet and, not wanting to be rude, she bowed in return. The cockatoo flew onto the Maharajah's shoulder with a loud squawk.

'Ah, yes,' the Maharajah went on. 'And this delightful creature is my Maharani. You see, Maharani is the name of a Maharajah's wife, and as I have never found a lady I could love as much as my darling bird, I call her my

Maharani.' With that, the cockatoo walked down his arm and sat on his wrist.

'How-d'ya-do? How-d'ya-do? How-d'ya-do?' she squawked at Violet.

Violet burst out laughing and replied, 'Very well, thank you. My name is Violet Remy-Robinson and I am delighted to meet you all.'

'I am delighted to meet you too,' the Maharajah said. 'I have heard all about you and your godmother from Hari. Hari is a good friend of mine and does such important work at the orphanage. Have you enjoyed your time in India, Violet?'

'It's all been amazing,' she replied, her eyes shining with pleasure, but then images of her parents and her cat, Pudding, floated through her mind, making her add quickly, 'but I'll be pleased to get home.' Violet felt something touching her and found the Maharani was gently nudging her.

'Oh, look, she likes you!' the Maharajah exclaimed with delight. 'Would you like to hold her? Put your wrist next to mine and see if she will come to you.'

Violet did so, and the parrot walked across.

'You are very honoured,' the Maharajah laughed. 'She will hardly go to anyone other than me. And certainly not this person,' he said, indicating towards a small, chubby lady, wearing a pair of tight white jeans, a bright, frilly blouse, and a good deal of make-up and jewellery, who was teetering towards them on very high heels.

'Angel, my dear.' The Maharajah greeted the lady kindly, but a little wearily. 'Come and meet my new young friend, Violet.' He turned to Violet. 'Angel is my late brother's daughter. We are each other's only family, so Angel lives here with me. She's hoping to become an actress, aren't you, Angel, my dear?'

The Maharani, still perched on Violet's wrist, began to squawk, 'She's no angel, she's no angel, she's no angel.' Violet noticed Rajesh trying to hide a smirk.

Angel glanced with obvious disinterest at Violet, before narrowing her eyes at the Maharani. 'Stupid bird!' she hissed.

'Now, now, ladies,' the Maharajah soothed. 'Please, no fighting. Not on New Year's Eve.

Now I just have to try some of this delicious food.' And, as if by magic, Rajesh appeared by his side with a plate piled high with the various dishes. The Maharajah turned to Violet and Angel again. 'Come, let us go and eat. Shall we find your godmother, Violet? I am such a fan of hers that I am worried I may get starstruck.'

Angel's ears pricked up. 'Is your godmother famous, Violet? Is she a celebrity?'

'Oh, no,' Violet explained, as they made their way over to Celeste, who was sat at one of the tables that had been placed in the garden for the party. 'She's just a photographer.'

'Just a photographer!' the Maharajah

exclaimed. 'She is one of the finest photographers in the world.'

They sat down next to Celeste, who greeted them all with her usual wide smile.

'My uncle says you are a photographer. Do you take photos of famous people?' Angel asked her excitedly.

'Not if I can help it,' Celeste explained with a laugh. 'I'm a wildlife photographer.'

Angel's face fell. 'What, like, animals?' she asked, her voice suggesting that she thought this was a deeply boring thing to do.

'Did you take some wonderful photos of the tigers?' the Maharajah asked Celeste. 'I am so pleased that you are going to bring some attention to their troubles. Please, will you tell me all about your trip?'

Later, when the sun had set and everyone had finished eating and drinking, the Maharajah announced that he would be honoured to show everyone his art collection.

'We can then gather back here to see the New Year in. But, Violet,' he said, 'you might find my art rather boring. Since the Maharani has taken such a shine to you, why don't you go with her and explore my garden? Rajesh will join you.'

The garden was a magical place, full of splashing fountains and dark pools filled with water lilies and fat, gliding goldfish.

Fireflies darted around and the thrum of crickets filled the air, punctuated by shouts and laughter from the streets beyond the high walls.

The garden had been brightly lit for the party with torches stuck in the ground like spears. In the corner, next to one of the high walls, there was a particularly ancient and gnarled banyan tree that was full of chattering monkeys, and it was towards this tree that Rajesh and Violet found themselves slowly walking, as they chatted away, the Maharani still perched on Violet's shoulder. They were not far from the tree when the peace in the garden was shattered by a fire cracker soaring over the walls and landing right at their feet with a bang like a gunshot. Startled, the Maharani let out a terrified squeal and flew off Violet's shoulder, circling around the sky squawking and screeching, before settling at the very top of the tree.

'Oh, no! Oh, dear!' Rajesh exclaimed. 'That is very bad. We must get her down before the Maharajah comes back, otherwise he will be very worried and upset – and that is not good for his heart. Here, Your Majesty! Here Your Ladyship! Please come here!' he called desperately. But the Maharani just gave him a withering look and turned away.

'Goodness me, what a disaster!' Rajesh fretted. 'Please, Violet, will you wait here and watch her in case she flies somewhere else, while I go and fetch some of her food?'

'I could climb up and get her if you like,' Violet offered.

'No, no please do not do such a thing. The monkeys can be very vicious and I wouldn't want you to fall from the tree. Please just stay here and watch her – I will be back in a minute.'

With that, Rajesh hurried off, leaving Violet suddenly feeling very alone in the large, night-time garden. She had seen plenty of monkeys while she'd been in India

and hadn't thought them scary. But now, as they all sat staring at her from the tree with their round eyes, Violet found herself feeling nervous. She tried not to look at them, but that was easier said than done, as she was supposed to be keeping an eye on the Maharani. Then one monkey jumped down from the tree and moved towards her, followed by another, and then another,

and before she knew what was happening,
she was surrounded. With panic rising in her
tummy, Violet looked desperately towards
the palace to see if Rajesh was returning – but
there was no sign of him.

Maybe I should run, she thought. But if she
ran, it might startle the monkeys and they
might attack her . . . Then, just as Violet was
wondering what to do, the monkeys began

to shriek at her. The noise was deafening and Violet was terrified. She was about to scream for help when there was a flurry of feathers and squawking and the Maharani swooped down, brave as a golden eagle, sending the monkeys scattering.

'Oh, thank you! Thank you so much!' Violet cried to the cockatoo, as she came and landed gently on Violet's wrist.

'Bad monkey,' the bird replied in a matter-of-fact tone of voice.

A moment later, Rajesh appeared, a green tin of food in his hand.

'Oh!' he cried. 'She has come down to you. How amazing!'

'She's an amazing bird,' Violet replied, gently stroking the cockatoo's head, while the Maharani cooed with pleasure.

2

INTRODUCING ART

HAPPY NEW YEAR

As she walked through the arrivals gate at the airport, Violet saw her parents waiting eagerly for her, clutching huge *Happy New Year* and *Welcome Home* banners. They couldn't wait to hear all about Violet and Celeste's Indian adventure and asked her lots and lots of questions the whole way home.

Pudding the cat, was sitting anxiously by the front door of their flat, waiting for Violet's safe return, and Norma had made

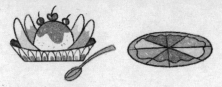

her favourite meal of cheese and tomato pizza, followed by a banana split.

But all too soon India seemed like a fantastically exciting, delightfully warm dream. A couple of days later, the Christmas holidays were over and Violet was being woken early one dark morning to get ready for school. Even the smell of Norma's freshly baked banana muffins didn't make getting up any easier. But, as so often happens with school, once Violet got there and saw her best friend Rose and all her other friends, it wasn't so bad.

Rose had spent Christmas and New Year staying with her family in Ireland, which she said she had loved, even if it wasn't quite as exciting as India. The girls hadn't seen each other since Violet got back, and Rose's eyes grew wide and her breath ragged at Violet's (rather exaggerated) tales of charging elephants, vicious sharp-toothed tigers that padded around their tent at night, and of course her narrow escape from the monkeys.

When Violet arrived home after school she found a note from her friend and neighbour, Dee Dee Derota, waiting for her.

Violet was curious. To whom could Dee Dee want to introduce her? Perhaps she had got a new cat? Lullabelle, her existing, extremely spoilt Persian cat would be furious.

Dearest Violet,
Happy new year! Please will you and Rose come to tea this afternoon. I want to hear all about your holidays – and there is someone I would like you to meet.
Fondest love,
Dee Dee ××××

She wandered out into the chilly garden to look for Rose, so they could go straight to Dee Dee's house and solve the mystery. She found her friend practising her ballet pliés on the lawn, using the back of a bench as a barre.

'Look, Violet, there's a new boy in the garden. He's over there, playing football – and he's really good. Stanley's furious,' Rose said.

Violet looked and saw a scraggy-looking boy with spiky red hair and pale freckly skin, perfectly heading a ball to one of the other boys. Stanley, Rose's older brother, was looking on enviously. The boy looked like he was the same age as Rose and Violet, and was wearing a red-and-white football shirt over a pair of purple shorts, which Violet recognised as the school colours of Fetherington's School for Young Gentlemen, an extremely grand school nearby. At that moment, the other team scored a goal and the red-headed boy let out a groan. Violet chuckled to herself before telling Rose about Dee Dee's invitation for tea, and they walked over to the old lady's flat.

Since Dee Dee had sold the Pearl of the Orient she had been on a Caribbean cruise, and her flat had been transformed by a very bossy lady called Lavinia, who had a blonde ponytail

and pointy glasses. She was a de-clutterer, or a Dee-Dee-clutterer, as Dee Dee had joked. Lavinia had hit the flat like a hurricane of tidiness and organisation and, after a week, all was transformed. Dee Dee's cupboards were a work of colour coordination, all her shoes had been neatly stacked in pairs, her make-up and nail varnishes were beautifully arranged on glass shelves in the bathroom, and her jewellery was no longer kept in a biscuit tin but a smart purple leather box with lots of drawers. And Lavinia didn't stop at tidying the flat. Oh no, she organised an endless stream of manicurists, cupcake deliveries, hairdressers, cat groomers, dry cleaners, yoga

teachers and anybody else she could think of to come to the flat to ensure that Dee Dee's life ran entirely smoothly. And it did, therefore Dee Dee was delighted.

So, Rose and Violet were surprised at the chaotic sight that greeted them as they walked into Dee Dee's flat that afternoon.

In the middle of the sitting room carpet was a mound of skateboards, footballs, a bike, a half-unpacked suitcase, a large pile of dirty washing, and several pairs of muddy football boots and trainers. The girls looked at Dee Dee with puzzled faces as she offered them a cup of tea and a French Fancy.

'Rose, Violet, I have had a very eventful time while you two were away,' she said. 'I don't know if I have ever told you about my brother, Burt? Well, perhaps not, because to be honest we don't always get on and he's not the best sort. But he is my family, and so is his son, Reggie - who I'm afraid rather takes after his father and as a result is being detained at His Majesty's pleasure.' Neither Rose or Violet knew what that meant, but they didn't like to interrupt. 'Reggie married a sweet girl called Jacintha and they had a son called Arthur. I have always helped them when I can . . .' The girls nodded away, wondering how any of this was connected to the pile of mess on Dee Dee's floor. 'Anyway, to cut a very long story short, Jacintha has gone travelling around the world to find herself – whatever that means – and Arthur has come to stay with me while she's away.'

Before either girl could reply, the back door was flung open and in came the red-haired boy from the garden. He was clutching a football to his chest, as if it were a precious jewel.

'And here he is!' Dee Dee announced. 'Art, this is Violet and Rose – who live on the garden too and are my particular friends.'

'Hello,' said Art, twirling the football on the end of his finger. 'Auntie, do you have any food? I'm absolutely starving!'

She passed him the plate of cakes. 'Now, did you find some other children to play football with in the garden?'

Art helped himself to four French Fancies (one lemon, two chocolate and one strawberry) and began to eat them as quickly as he could. With his mouth full of cake, he answered Dee Dee's question. 'I did play a game and everyone was nice – except this one boy who seemed really mean. Every time I had the ball he looked at me like . . .' Then he did a perfect imitation of Stanley's grumpy face. 'He was a right—' The girls burst out laughing, as Dee Dee interrupted Art swiftly.

'Stanley is Rose's brother, Artie dear. And please don't talk with your mouth full.'

Art flushed as pink with embarrassment as the French Fancy he was eating. 'I'm really sorry.'

'It's all right,' Rose said. 'He's not very nice to me either.'

'So have you just started at Fetherington's?' Violet asked, pointing at his clothes.

Art nodded, looking very unimpressed.

'Poor Art didn't have the best first day,

but I'm sure it will get better. Everyone says it's a wonderful school – and they were so kind finding him a place at the last minute,' Dee Dee said, cheerfully.

Art continued to look glum. 'There's not much sport and no drama, which are the only things that make school okay. It's just weird things like Ancient Greek and loads of maths,' he said to Violet and Rose, who nodded sympathetically.

'Now Rose is our rising ballet star, aren't you, darlin'?' Dee Dee said. 'When will they will be holding auditions for this year's Easter show? I simply adore the Easter ballet show they do – it's at a proper theatre in the

West End and is just such a treat.' Dee Dee explained to Art, 'Rose kindly invited me to watch her in *Swan Lake* last year and she was marvellous. And this year, Rose, I'm sure you'll get the star role!'

'I think the auditions will be next week.' Rose swallowed nervously. She wanted the lead part so much that it sent her into a panic just thinking about it. The ballet was *Sleeping Beauty*. Every night she lay in bed, picturing herself walking up to the notice board at school, and reading the cast list in Madame's neat handwriting – and then the perfect joy of seeing:

PRINCESS AURORA
TO BE PLAYED BY
ROSE TRELAWNEY

The alarm on Violet's watch went off, breaking the spell.

'What's that?' Art asked, puzzled.

'It's my watch alarm to tell me to go home, so I'm not late for my supper,' Violet explained.

And then from outside they heard the sound of Rose's mother calling her name.

'And that's my alarm!' Rose said with a smile.

'Well, then you must hurry along, girls. But I am so pleased you've met Art – and you must make sure you come back very soon and tell me all about your holidays.'

The girls promised to return, and dashed home in opposite directions for supper.

One Saturday morning at the beginning of February, the Remy-Robinsons were eating breakfast together. Violet was sharing a stack of banana pancakes with Pudding, Camille was eating a bowl of mango, and Benedict was munching away on a piece of toast and marmalade while he read the newspaper.

'Oh dear! That's very sad,' he suddenly announced.

'What?' Camille and Violet asked in unison.

'I'm afraid, Violet, that your friend the

43

Maharajah of Bochir has died. There are pictures here of his magnificent funeral.' Benedict showed them the article in the paper. There was a picture of the Maharajah as a younger man with the Maharani sitting on his shoulder, and then photos of his funeral with crowds of people dressed in white, together with a parade of elephants.

'That is sad,' Violet agreed, feeling upset. 'He was a very nice man.'

'It says that he died peacefully in his sleep,' Benedict went on. 'And he was ninety-two, which is an extremely good age. And then it goes on to say that he was a very eccentric

man and, true to character, he has left a very unusual will.'

'What's a will?' Violet asked.

'A will is a bit like a letter in which you say what you want done with all your things when you die,' Benedict explained. 'Your friend the Maharajah has left everything, with the exception of some money he's given to his niece and various servants, in the charge of the Maharani, who is a cockatoo! And the bird has to decide who gets the Maharajah's fortune. This is the Maharani sitting on his shoulder, presumably?'

'That's right,' Violet said. 'Do you remember

I told you about her? She scared away the monkeys for me. She's amazing.'

'Amazing she may be,' her father replied. 'But perhaps not the best choice to be left in charge of a fortune, which is estimated here to be - wow, an awful lot. It says that the Maharani holds the "secret" to the hidden treasure. I wonder what that means?'

'Your godmother Celeste will know what is happening,' Camille said. 'We can ask her, although I think that at the moment she is in the South Pole, photographing penguins.'

'Oh, Pudding, you've eaten all my pancakes,' Violet exclaimed crossly, looking down at her empty plate. Pudding slunk away guiltily, his tummy gently swaying beneath him.

Celeste arrived in London a few days later. She was on a very short stop-over on her way to Greenland, and, over a glass of champagne, she filled them in on all the news.

'Poor Hari. He is very worried about money because he completely relied on the Maharajah. Now he is using his own money to pay for the orphanage, but he can only afford to do that for a couple more months.'

'Oh dear! And what's all this about the cockatoo holding the "secret" to the treasure?' Benedict asked.

'Well, people are saying she knows how to find the fortune, but the bird has not spoken a word since the Maharajah died,' Celeste replied. 'Angel – who, by the way, is absolutely hopping mad about not being left the whole fortune – has been telling the newspapers that there have been several kidnap attempts on the bird. Everyone is so concerned that the Prime Minister of India has set a time limit – if the Maharani does not speak by the beginning of April all the money will go to the government.'

'Gosh,' Camille said. 'That's when Easter is this year, isn't it? Not long away at all.'

'Who is looking after the Maharani?' Violet asked Celeste.

'Rajesh was named as her guardian in the will, so she's in safe hands at least.'

Violet nodded in agreement. Rajesh would be kind to the Maharani, but the poor thing must be missing the Maharajah dreadfully. And what would happen to the orphans if she didn't speak soon?

A couple of weeks later, on a dark and stormy night – which also happened to be Valentine's Day – Violet, feeling cosy in her bedroom, was getting ready for bed. She was talking to Pudding, who was curled up on her pillow as usual, when the doorbell rang. Camille and Benedict had gone out for dinner so Norma was babysitting. She was making a special Valentine's cake for Ernest and was just in the middle of a tricky piece of icing. She called out to Violet to see who was at the door, and said that she would come in a moment.

Violet ran downstairs and, as Norma had taught her to do, looked through the spyhole in the front door to see who was there. And when she did, she couldn't believe her eyes. For there, sheltering under an enormous umbrella, was Rajesh and a very grumpy-looking Maharani. Violet opened the door immediately.

'Rajesh! Whatever are you doing here? You must come in out of the rain.'

'Please, Miss Violet, will you look after the Maharani? I have taken her away from Miss Angel because she is being so cruel to her and also I think it is not safe for her in Bochir. Miss Angel keeps talking about dangerous criminals trying to kidnap the Maharani. Please, no one will ever think to look here. It will just be for a month and then I will return. Now I must leave in case I am being followed.'

And with that, he thrust the shivering, wet cockatoo at Violet, together with a tin of Fortnum and Mason fruit and nut mix.

'That is the only food the Maharani will eat,' Rajesh explained.

Violet took both without really thinking and, before she could protest, Rajesh ran out to a waiting taxi which immediately drove off.

When Norma arrived a moment later, she found Violet looking confused, holding a cockatoo and a pale green tin.

At that moment, another taxi drew up and out got her parents. When they saw Violet and the Maharani they were as amazed as Norma. Questions hit Violet from all sides.

'WHY ON EARTH HAVE YOU GOT A PARROT, VIOLET? WHERE DID IT COME FROM?'

'SHE'S A COCKATOO.'

'ISN'T THAT THE MAHARAJAH'S COCKATOO?'

GROWL!

'I HATE COCKATOOS!'

'I THINK SHE IS RATHER BEAUTIFUL.'

HISS!

SQUAWK!

HISS!

'BUT WHY IS SHE HERE?'

'SHE'S STAYING FOR HOW LONG? A MONTH!'

'I'M SURE I'M ALLERGIC TO IT. I CAN FEEL MY NOSE ITCHING.'

SQUAWK!

'WHAT'S THIS TIN OF FOOD? WHAT DO YOU MEAN SHE ONLY EATS FOOD FROM FORTNUM AND MASON? OH, HONESTLY, I HAVE NEVER HEARD OF ANYTHING SO RIDICULOUS IN MY LIFE.'

GROWL!

'SHH, YOU'LL UPSET HER! COCKATOOS ARE VERY INTELLIGENT. AND THEY CAN TALK.'

'GREAT, I LOOK FORWARD TO LOTS OF INTELLECTUAL DISCUSSIONS.'

'I THINK IT IS A NICE VALENTINE'S SURPRISE.'

HISS!!

Just to add to the general chaos, Pudding also appeared, looked horrified and let out an almighty *hiss*. The Maharani gave an exaggerated *squawk* and buried her head in Violet's neck, which made Pudding even more furious. 'I'm with Pudding on this,' Benedict announced, and stomped back into the flat.

As Violet had no way of contacting Rajesh, the Maharani had to stay. But oh dear, Benedict and Pudding did find the cockatoo very annoying. The bird decided Violet's bedroom was her new home, evicting a furious Pudding and using the end of Violet's bed as a perch. She then refused to leave that room.

The heating had to be turned up full all day, otherwise she made a sort of squawking and shivering noise which Benedict, who worked at home, found more irritating than being boiling hot. So he started wearing shorts and a T-shirt instead of his usual suit, with Pudding (who was secretly pleased about the heating) sitting all over his drawings in his office.

Violet loved having the Maharani to stay, but did feel bad about Pudding. She tried to be totally fair, spending equal time with each of them, and she lectured both of them about learning to get on. It didn't work. And the rest of the time she spent trying to persuade the Maharani to talk. It was so important for the orphans, she explained patiently to the bird, but the Maharani just turned the other way and sulked.

Only Camille remained as serene as ever. And the Maharani loved Camille almost as much as she loved Violet, and would allow her to stroke and pet her, while Benedict and Pudding looked on, fuming.

4

A CAN OF COKE

PUDDING'S PLAN

It was only a few days later when Violet had another unexpected visitor.

'Surprise!' Angel exclaimed, tottering unsteadily on the doorstep in high-heeled furry boots. Ignoring Norma, who had opened the door to her, she kissed Violet extravagantly on both cheeks. 'How are you, Violet darling? I thought I simply must look you up since I was in London and we got on so amazingly well at the New Year's Eve party.'

Violet was speechless. A bewildered hello

was all she could manage in reply, as Norma escaped back to the kitchen.

'Well, aren't you going to invite me in?' Angel asked, peering over Violet's shoulder into the flat.

Violet hesitated. She couldn't let Angel see the Maharani, who was in her bedroom with the door wide open. But Violet couldn't very well refuse Angel without seeming very rude. So she found herself replying, 'Er, yes of course. Can I get you a drink?' she offered, leading Angel into the sitting room.

'I would love a Coke,' Angel replied, flopping down on to the sofa, nearly sitting on Pudding. The cat let out a cross miaow and

leaped out of the way just in time.

Angel eyed Pudding with distaste.

'I'm, like, totally allergic to cats, so would you mind moving it out of the room?'

Oh drat, Violet thought, but she tried very hard not to look annoyed.

'Of course, that's fine. I'll be right back.'

Violet whizzed off, clutching a grumpy Pudding. She didn't dare check on the Maharani in case it set her off squawking.

So she just delivered Pudding into the kitchen, quickly explaining who Angel was to Norma and asking that she please, please keep Pudding in the kitchen and away from the Maharani. A Coke can and a glass in her hands, she returned to the sitting room at top speed, shutting the door behind her.

'So, sweetie, what have you been up to?' Angel asked, grabbing the Coke and ripping the top off it.

Violet never knew what to say when people asked her that.

'Um, you know, school and stuff,' she replied. 'I am really sorry about your uncle's death.'

Angel shrugged. 'He was like really, really old. The real tragedy is how badly he has treated me. I'm sure you have heard, it has been in all the newspapers.'

Violet nodded politely, saying, 'It's terrible for the orphans too, I know. My godmother said—'

'The orphans?' Angel interrupted. 'The orphans are used to being poor. I'm not. When I think of all the years I have selflessly neglected my career as an actress to be his companion! I had top Bollywood directors begging, literally begging, me to star in their films.' She gave a long sigh and took a big gulp of Coke. 'Anyway, I know this must seem a strange question to ask, Violet darling, but I don't suppose you have seen the Maharani, have you?'

Violet felt herself go bright red as Angel looked at her intently. Violet hated lying, but she knew that, at moments such as this, it was entirely necessary. So she gave it her best shot.

'No, no, not at all,' she replied innocently. 'Isn't she in India with Rajesh?'

Angel was looking at Violet very suspiciously. 'No, Violet, she's not. She was with me, but then Rajesh kidnapped her, bringing her to England. He said it was to keep her safe, but I'm sure he just wants the fortune for himself.'

Violet was about to defend Rajesh and say that she thought that the Maharajah had left the Maharani in his care, but she stopped herself. She just shook her head and repeated that she hadn't seen Rajesh or the Maharani.

'Okay. Well, I think I'm done here,' Angel said, getting to her feet.

Violet opened the sitting-room door and ushered Angel out into the hall, just as Pudding was escaping from the kitchen. Oh dear! It was like watching an accident happen in slow motion. Pudding took one look at Angel, turned and ran the other way into . . . you guessed it, Violet's bedroom.

GROWL!

SQUAWK!

HISS!!..

Angel raised one eyebrow at Violet. 'Are you sure you haven't seen the Maharani?' she asked, in not a very nice way.

Violet thought very, very quickly.

'Oh, no, no, that's not the Maharani. That's er . . . er Desdemona, my very own cockatoo. I got her because I loved the Maharani so much. She and my cat hate each other – it's a nightmare!' Violet gabbled.

'Can I meet her?' Angel asked slyly.

'Er, afraid not, no, she's terribly shy and can be quite vicious too. She might go for your eyes or claw your face,' Violet replied quickly.

'I see,' Angel said thoughtfully before adding briskly, 'Thanks for the drink, Violet. See you around.'

Phew, thought Violet, shutting the door behind her. *I'm glad I got away with that.*

lots of
make-up

There was great excitement among the garden children. Someone had moved into the house that had once been lived in by the Du Plicitous family. All anyone knew was that she was a woman with long hair who always wore dark glasses and a lot of make-up. Apparently she never came into the garden and she had only been glimpsed through the windows. Lydia spread the rumour that she was a witch with the magical power to turn people to stone, while Matthew decided she was a reclusive movie star who had had plastic surgery that had gone terribly wrong, whilst Violet thought maybe she was the Count's long-lost sister who had been held captive for years by bandits in South America but had recently escaped. Art, who had been fully absorbed into the 'midders' group in the garden (even managing to get on with Stanley), spun an elaborate tale that she was a dangerous con-artist on the run from the police. Stanley terrified all the littilees (and some older children), with an incredibly gory tale of her being a flesh-eating zombie, who roamed around the garden at night looking for prey. The woman, he said, had been satisfying her appetite with small mice and birds, but it was only a matter of time before she munched on the cats, and then, when she had eaten all of those, it seemed logical that she would turn to small children.

Only sensible Rose thought to ask Ernest who the lady was. She spotted him in the garden, one sunny Saturday, chatting with Norma. Ernest listened to all the ideas with a smile on his face and then said, 'Any one of those ideas might be true. All I know is that she is a friend of a friend of the Countess's and she is paying them a lot of rent for just one room. I don't really see her; she stays

69

in her room, doesn't ever allow me in there,
goes out when I do and always locks her door.'

One March evening, Violet and Rose were
walking across the dark garden to Rose's house.
Despite having spent the whole day together
at school and having walked home together,
there still seemed a huge amount to discuss.
And the main thing was that ROSE HAD
BEEN CHOSEN TO PLAY PRINCESS
AURORA IN *SLEEPING BEAUTY*! Violet
was delighted for her friend and Rose was so
excited and nervous that she could hardly
think straight.

Anyway, where were we? Oh yes, so the

two girls were walking briskly across the garden trying not to think about Stanley's tales of flesh-eating zombies, flashing their torches from side to side, when, to their great alarm, they heard a strange noise coming from one of the bushes. They both froze, listening. It was a strange, snuffling noise, but Violet quickly decided it didn't sound like a zombie.

'Do you think one of the cats has hurt itself?' Violet whispered.

Rose didn't answer. She was too busy being terrified by the pictures of strange, snuffling zombies filling her head. She would have run, except she couldn't move.

'Stay here, I'll just go and check,' Violet said. Rose would have objected, on the grounds it was far too dangerous, but at that moment she was too scared to speak, so instead she made a sort of mewling noise, which Violet (mistakenly) took as agreement.

As Violet came close to the bush, her torch shining like a beacon in front of her, the noise stopped abruptly. *Better still check,* she thought. So she did. And imagine her surprise when she found not an injured cat, but Art – looking very embarrassed with a tear-stained face.

'Are you okay?' Violet asked kindly. 'Has something happened at school?'

Art nodded, swallowing hard.

Rose, who was listening, decided that zombies didn't often go to school, and arrived just as Violet was offering round a bag of Norma's homemade toffees that she had stowed in her pocket. They both took one gratefully and, after a moment's steady chewing, Art began to explain.

'I got into a fight with this boy and Mr Smith, the geography teacher, who hates me anyway, said it was all my fault, which it wasn't, and he sent me to the headmaster who rang Auntie Dee Dee - and now . . .' Art nearly started crying again, his face puckering, '. . . and now she's really upset. And she's been so kind, and I love living here - it's like having a proper home - and I feel really guilty, but I just hate it at school.' He wiped his nose on his jumper sleeve.

Violet nodded, but Rose, with a wisdom beyond her years, said, 'I know it's a very good school, but I think it's the wrong school for you.'

Art shrugged. 'But Auntie's been so generous

paying for me to go, and everyone in the family was so excited about it. My mum said it's a "once-in-a-lifetime" opportunity for me, going to such a good school. I can be a doctor or a lawyer, she says. But I'm just not good at anything there – it's all really academic stuff, which I just can't get. I'm not clever. And I'm not even good at art – the teacher tore up all my work, he said it was so bad.'

'How mean!' said Violet.

'You're really good at football,' Rose added.

'But they don't even play football; they play rugby, which I'm useless at.'

'You're very good at imitating people,' Violet said.

'I know, and I thought it would be a way to make the other boys like me a bit. So I did imitations of all the teachers one breaktime, but then someone told on me. I got called to the staff room to show the teachers. They didn't see the funny side at all, so I got detentions for a week.'

Oh, dear, what to do? The girls couldn't really see an easy solution so Violet handed round more toffees and they chewed in sympathetic silence.

Something strange was happening that was bothering Norma in more ways than the obvious. A couple of weeks after the Maharani's arrival, many more people than normal had started coming to the front door.

It began on a Tuesday. At half past nine, a window cleaner rang the doorbell, offering to wash the windows at an incredibly low price. They had only been washed the week before, so Norma sent him away. At quarter past eleven, a man arrived wanting to come into the flat to interview Norma for a survey. Norma was much too busy so she politely refused. At three, just as Norma was leaving to pick up Violet from school, a woman appeared on the doorstep wanting to fill her freezer with fresh fish. And when Norma said no thank you, she walked off in a fury. The next day, Norma had just finished clearing up breakfast, when the doorbell rang and a man tried, very insistently, to come in and talk to her about insurance. She sent him away, only for the doorbell to go an hour later, with another man from the electricity board wanting to read the meter. She let him in and showed him the meter cupboard

9.30AM

11.15AM

3PM

NEXT DAY

I HOUR LATER

in the hall. She went back to the kitchen to do her work but then heard such a squawking from the Maharani that she came running to find the meter man in Violet's bedroom and the Maharani flying around the ceiling. The meter man mumbled, 'Nice parrot,' and ran off.

Benedict appeared out of his office. 'What is going on?'

'I don't know,' replied Norma, truthfully, because at that moment she was still completely puzzled. But by the next day, when the doorbell had continued ringing practically every hour, she had a pretty good idea.

So that evening, when Camille, Benedict and Violet were all gathered together in the sitting room, chatting away over cocktails (or apple juice, in Violet's case), Norma went in to announce her suspicions.

'I don't wish to worry you, but I think someone is trying to steal the Maharani.'

Violet gasped and Camille gave a horrified, '*Mon Dieu!* Are you sure?'

Norma explained her suspicions.

'Why bother to steal her?' Benedict asked. 'I will gladly give her to anyone who asks.'

Violet and Camille both shot him dirty looks.

'I was only joking,' he said, taking a large gulp of his cocktail.

'This is very serious. I must ring PC Green,' Camille said.

PC Green was a friend of Violet's whom she had met when she was solving the mystery of the Pearl of the Orient. He often popped round for a chat and to get her advice on cases. He was very nice, but Violet didn't think he was the best at solving crimes, so announced, 'I had better go and find Rose.'

But Rose was out at rehearsals until late that evening, and most of the following day too, so Violet left her a rather bossy note saying:

URGENT DETECTIVE WORK!!!!
CRIME—SOLVING NEEDED. Someone is trying to steal the Maharani!! Please come and find me the minute you get home!!!
LOVE VIOLET xxxxxx

PC Green was there when she got back, taking down the details in his notebook, while polishing off a plate of Norma's delicious flapjacks. He listened to Norma as she told him all about her visitors.

'And the strangest thing is,' she said, 'that they all look rather alike, even though they are all ages, and men and women. Almost as if—'

'They were related!' PC Green jumped in. 'It'll be a family of criminals who've read about the parrot and tracked her here. Could be dangerous for you. Do you want me to take the bird down the station to protect her? I could put her in one of the cells. No one would get her there.'

'No!' Violet said. 'No, she would hate that – and besides, I promised Rajesh I would look after her.'

'We will just have to be very careful about who we let into the flat,' Camille said.

'Absolutely,' PC Green agreed. 'Maybe you should have a password? I mean you just let me in.'

'But we know you,' Benedict said, a puzzled look on his face.

'Good point,' said PC Green. 'I can see these criminals won't be fooling you. Well, best of luck – and let me know if there is anything else I can do.'

The following day was Saturday, and Violet's godfather, Johnny, was due to arrive in London to stay with them. He spent most of his time travelling around the world playing in poker championships. It was Johnny who had taught Violet to play poker one hot afternoon when they had all been on holiday together. They had both been surprised at how good she was. Johnny and Violet's father had been best friends since they were small boys and this seemed to mean that they had to behave like small boys whenever they saw each other.

Benedict, Violet and Camille met Johnny at his favourite Chinese restaurant for lunch.

'I cannot believe you've got this famous parrot living with you!' Johnny spluttered, over a mouthful of spring roll. 'I've just been in Kuala Lumpur and the newspapers there have been absolutely full of stories of the Maharani's disappearance and the Maharajah's will. And all the time she has been living in your bedroom, Violet! Have you got her to tell you the secret of the Maharajah's fortune yet?'

Violet shook her head. 'She hasn't spoken since she's been with us.'

'I think the poor bird is very traumatised by the Maharajah's death,' Camille said.

Benedict made a sort of hurrumphing noise. 'She's the most, spoilt, pig-headed creature I have ever come across.'

Johnny laughed. 'Well, I can't wait to meet her,' he said, and then whispered to Violet, 'I've been giving some thought to your poker training. I think you should master Texas Hold 'Em.'

Camille heard him. 'Can't you play chess with Violet?' she protested. 'She's very good at that.'

'But *I'm* not. Don't worry, we'll only be playing for matches. And besides, I'm sure

Violet will grow up to be a very respectable and highly successful young lady, but there is no harm in having a little fun now and then. Besides, poker is a very good way to improve your maths and . . . communication skills.' And he gave Violet a solemn wink and poured Camille a large glass of plum wine.

They all arrived back home stuffed full of delicious food. While Camille and Benedict made tea, Violet took Johnny to her bedroom to meet the Maharani. But disaster had struck . . . When Violet opened the bedroom door she found the window wide open and the Maharani gone!

Violet checked under the bed, while Johnny told Camille and Benedict. They appeared in the doorway, looking very worried, and both started talking at once.

'Have you found her?'

'Did you leave the window open?'

'Are you sure you didn't?'

'Someone must have broken in!'

'How terrible!'

'You go and check in the garden, just in case, while I ring PC Green,' said Camille.

PC Green got very overexcited and put out a national alert to the all the airports and ferry terminals to be on the lookout for a cockatoo. He promised to come round later to examine the crime scene.

Meanwhile in the garden, Rose and Art helped Violet search for the Maharani. But there was no trace of the cockatoo. They examined the window and the flowerbeds below it for clues, and got very excited by the discovery of some muddy footprints and a couple of squashed flowers. But, as Rose pointed out, that didn't really tell them who had taken the Maharani.

PC Green arrived and, after scratching his head a little, said that he was sure it was the family of criminals that had been bothering Norma. 'They'll be miles away by now,' he added cheerfully. Of course, this only made Violet feel worse.

The light was fading, so everyone made their way back inside except Violet, who lingered a little longer in the garden, sadly shaking the tin of food in the middle of the lawn, unable to bear the thought of losing the Maharani.

'Bye Violet,' Art said. 'I hope you find her.' And he wandered back to Dee Dee's flat.

'Come on, Violet,' her mother called to her.

'Don't look so glum, chérie, I'm sure the Maharani will be found. Why doesn't Rose stay for a sleepover?'

After a cheering supper of spaghetti bolognese and chocolate mousse, Rose and Violet both had a bath and got into their pyjamas.

'Shall we draw a crime-solving matrix?' Rose suggested. 'It worked for finding the Pearl of the Orient, so I'm sure it will work here,' she added optimistically.

Violet agreed and they began. They filled in the crime part easily, but then when it came to suspects they were stumped, apart from PC Green's idea of a criminal family.

CRIME TO SOLVE - THE KIDNAPPING OF THE MAHARANI

WHERE DID THE CRIME TAKE PLACE?
In Violet's bedroom, while she was out for lunch with her parents.

WERE THERE ANY WITNESSES TO THE CRIME?
No

WHAT CLUES WERE THERE?
Muddy footprints and trampled flowers.

WHAT CONCLUSIONS CAN BE DRAWN FROM THIS?
That someone broke into Violet's bedroom from the garden.

DO THEY HAVE A MOTIVE?
Yes, the Maharajah's fortune.

DO THESE DETAILS MATCH ANY SUSPECTS?
Maybe a criminal family.

IF SO, DO THEY HAVE ANY ALIBI?
Not known.

DOES THIS LEAD YOU TO ANY SENSIBLE CONCLUSIONS?
NO!!!!!!!!!!!! ....

Rose frowned. 'I really feel like we are missing something.'

'I agree, but what?' Violet asked with a sigh.

'Time for bed, girls,' Benedict announced, appearing in the doorway. 'Lights out now and no more chatting.'

For once they did as they were told and were both quickly fast asleep.

It was about eleven o'clock that night, when Violet woke up with a jolt. There was a noise – like heavy rain or hail hitting her window. But it wasn't. Someone was throwing stones at it.

She rushed over to see Art in the garden below, just visible in the pearly moonlight. She pushed up her window.

'What are you doing here?' Violet hissed down to him.

'I know where she is! The Maharani, I've found her!'

Violet lost no time. She woke Rose and they pulled on their clothes.

'Can you manage to climb down?' Violet asked Rose. Rose looked uncertain.

'I'm not very good at climbing, and especially not down drainpipes.'

'You will be fine,' Violet said, deciding for Rose. 'Don't worry about the drainpipe. I'll hold on tight to your arms and you can lower yourself down.

Then Art can help you at the bottom.'

It was all rather clumsy and embarrassing but Rose reached the bottom safely.

Violet shinned down the drainpipe in a flash.

'Wow,' Art said. 'You are good at climbing.'

Violet blushed a little at the compliment, as the girls followed him across the garden. He led them through Dee Dee's flat, which was silent except for the faint sound of the old lady's gentle snoring, and opened the door of what Violet had always assumed to be a cupboard. It was, in fact, an old flight of stairs up to the Du Plicitouses' house which was above Dee Dee's basement flat.

The three of them crept up it until they reached the locked door at the top. Art produced a piece of wire and proceeded to ease the lock until it clicked and he could open the door.

'Where did you learn to do that?' Violet asked, genuinely impressed.

'From my dad,' Art replied simply. 'Better not tell that policeman friend of yours,' he added with a smirk.

Violet thought of all the things that her father had taught her – how to bowl overarm in cricket, how to draw a straight line without a ruler – and frankly they didn't measure up. How incredibly useful would it be to know how to open a locked door with a piece of wire? That was a proper life skill, especially for someone as curious as Violet.

Once inside, they immediately heard a squawking sound coming from the second floor. Art put his finger to his lips, and together the three of them crept through the house, as silent as cats, towards the noise.

As they reached the upstairs landing, Violet noticed a bedroom door that was open a little, enabling them to peak through.

The Maharani was squawking and flapping around the ceiling, while Chiang-Mai, the Du Plicitouses' Siamese cat stood up on his hind legs, hissing and growling furiously.

Since the animals were alone, Violet, Rose and Art walked into the room. The Maharani gave a loud squawk of relief and landed on Violet's shoulder. Rose tried to pick up Chiang-Mai to comfort him, but he hissed at her and ran under the bed.

The bedroom looked extraordinary; like a fancy dress shop. All the walls were hung with an amazing variety of different outfits, from men's suits to flowery dresses, anoraks to old ladies' tweed coats, tracksuits to tuxedos. The dressing table was crowded with trays of make-up, false noses, jewellery, spectacles and mannequin heads wearing different wigs, moustaches and beards.

How very strange, thought Rose. What on earth could someone be doing with all these clothes?

But Violet was thinking about what Norma had said. All the people who came to the door were all in different clothes but somehow looked the same. An idea was forming in her head . . .

'What if . . .' Violet began, 'what if all the people were not a family, but the same person dressed up in different disguises?'

Both Art and Rose looked at her with great admiration.

'But who could that be?' Rose asked.

'One of the criminals who tried to kidnap the Maharani in India?' Art suggested.

'Maybe,' Violet said, but somehow that didn't feel like the right answer. She was just wondering to herself why it didn't when they heard footsteps on the stairs.

'Hide!' Art instructed and they all desperately looked around for suitable places – but it was too late. The door opened, revealing a lady with long blonde hair and huge sunglasses, carrying a large, greasy, newspaper package of what looked and smelled like fish and chips.

Violet might not have recognised the lady, had she not

whipped off her sunglasses and said furiously to her, 'Violet! How did you get in?'

'Angel,' Violet stammered. 'What am I doing here? What are you doing here?' And then it dawned on her. Of course! Who would have more reason to steal the Maharani?

'It was you,' Violet cried, 'dressing up as all those different people, trying to steal the Maharani!'

Angel shrugged. 'I am a brilliant actress, you know,' she replied.

'But how did you know that I had the Maharani?' Violet asked, genuinely amazed.

'Violet, you are not a good actress.

You must think I am stupid if you thought I'd fall for your nonsense about having your own cockatoo, who happened to sound exactly like the Maharani.'

'Oh,' Violet replied, as there didn't seem much else to say.

'So now,' Angel continued, 'I have merely taken back what is mine. Rajesh stole the Maharani from me and—'

But she was interrupted by Ernest popping his head around the door. 'Very urgent phone call for you, madam,' he announced.

Angel hesitated. She was waiting for an important phone call from a director about an audition. 'Don't you dare move,' she growled at the children. 'I'll be right back.' She put down her fish and chips, stomping past Ernest and down the stairs to the telephone.

'I'm not even going to ask you three what you are doing out of bed and how you got in here,' remarked Ernest. 'Now I'm guessing this is your missing bird? And she will come if you call her?'

Violet nodded as the Maharani came and perched on her shoulder.

'Right then,' Ernest said briskly and pushed up one of the sash windows. 'Put her out in the garden and then you can get her later.'

Violet hesitated.

'Trust me, Violet,' Ernest said. 'It's your best chance of getting her back.'

Reluctantly, Violet took the Maharani over to the window and flung her out.

Just at that moment, Angel returned. 'There was no one there,' she complained to Ernest. And then, when she saw the open window, she screamed at all of them, 'WHAT HAVE YOU DONE?'

Ernest played dumb. 'Oh, I'm so sorry, it was me. I thought the parrot must have got trapped in here somehow, so I opened the window to chase it out. Chiang-Mai was very upset. I'm very sorry if that was the wrong thing, I'll try to get it back.' He leaned out of the window and called in a half-hearted way: 'Here, parroty parroty . . . No, I'm sorry, it's gone. I'm sure she'll come back in the morning. Can I get you any tea?'

'No I don't want TEA!' she thundered. 'That's an incredibly valuable bird! The Count will hear of this!'

Ernest regarded her steadily. 'The Count and Countess hate parrots and I'm most sure they would not want one in their house, upsetting Chiang-Mai,' he replied coldly.

'Oh, get out, all of you!' she shouted rudely.

'Good night,' Ernest said politely, while the others dived through the door.

In the dark, silent garden, Violet called softly for the Maharani. Seconds later, the bird swooped down on to her shoulder. The Maharani didn't actually say thank you, but Violet could tell by the way she was nuzzling her neck that she was extremely relieved to be rescued.

From the window above, Angel watched, seething with rage. The parcel of fish and chips was wafting delicious smells at her.

I must eat, she told herself, *to keep my strength up*; so she sat down on her bed and began to munch her way through the contents. She was going to have to be much, much cleverer, she decided. She was an amazing actress after all, so it shouldn't be too difficult.

The following day, to celebrate the Maharani's rescue, Violet, Rose and Art were allowed to go to the nearby sweet shop on their own as a special treat.

As they walked past the Du Plicitouses' old house on the way, who should burst out the front door but Angel. She was dressed in a huge squashy fur coat with sunglasses perched on her head and a suitcase in each hand. Ignoring Rose and Art, she climbed down the stairs, calling, in her best dramatic voice: 'Violet, darling, what a coincidence! I just wanted to tell you that I am leaving for India this minute and to say how sorry I was for kidnapping the Maharani. It was truly a terrible thing to do and I can see now that I just wanted to hang on to some tiny reminder of my dear, beloved uncle.' And here she made a funny face as if she were trying to stop herself crying. 'I was so utterly devastated by his death.' She produced a tissue at this point and dabbed her dry eyes. Then she took a very deep breath. 'Anyway, I know I need to be brave and move on. So I have decided that I in order to get over my immense grief I must follow my dream. By an amazing coincidence, a top top film director rang this morning and begged me to be the leading lady in a huge, huge film. So wish me luck!'

'Good luck,' Violet muttered.

A taxi drew up beside them but Angel hadn't quite finished.

'And I know it's absolutely the best thing for the Maharani. She is so much safer with you. All those gangs of dangerous criminals probably won't even think of looking here.' Angel looked around the street, as if the gangs might be lurking behind cars, ready to pounce. She gave a little shudder. 'Terrifying – and such a huge responsibility. Awful. So I'm so pleased you are prepared to do it.

Thank you. Anyway, mustn't keep the cab waiting. Bye bye.'

And she loaded her suitcases into the taxi, as a mystified Violet replied, 'Okay, bye then.'

'Bye then,' Rose and Art echoed as they watched the taxi rumble off, leaving the trio standing on the pavement. They all found themselves looking anxiously up and down the street too. But it was entirely empty so they hurried off to the sweet shop, before any scary, dangerous criminals could appear.

10
THE IMPORTANCE OF A TWEED SUIT

February turned into March and those familiar signs of spring appeared: daffodils in the park and Easter eggs in the shops. Rose was incredibly busy rehearsing for *Sleeping Beauty* which was at the end of March, on Good Friday. And poor Art was still miserable at school and not doing very well, so Dee Dee (or rather Lavinia) had found him a tutor with whom he had spend a couple of hours after school every day. The only good thing was that Dee Dee was taking him to Jamaica at Easter to meet up with his mother, so he was very excited about that.

Therefore Violet spent a lot of her spare time either trying to persuade the Maharani to talk or playing poker with Johnny. She had mastered Texas Hold 'Em, and Johnny was now teaching her all he knew about the art of bluffing, as he called it. It was crucial, he explained, for poker, to pretend to have rubbish cards when in fact you have fantastic ones, and vice versa.

'It's all about the bluff, Violet,' he advised. 'It's all about the bluff.'

Norma was busy packing, as it was the time of year that she went home to visit her mother and father. While Norma was away visiting her parents, one of her nieces was to stand in for her, keeping the house tippity-top and collecting Violet from school. Her name was Jo, and Violet liked her because she bought her sweets and crisps after school every day, and let her do whatever she wanted. Camille and Benedict were less keen.

The day after Norma left, Violet returned home from school to find Johnny and her father drinking tea and eating walnut cake in the kitchen with Rajesh. The Maharani was sitting on Rajesh's shoulder. He had swapped his normal outfit for a three-piece tweed suit and a tweed cap.

'I have just been in the countryside visiting the Maharajah's old school friend, Colonel Smyth-Buntington,' Rajesh explained. 'He lives with his son and daughter-in-law, Simon and Fiona, in the beautiful Wiltshire countryside.

'And the good news is,' Benedict said, 'that Fiona loves birds and would be honoured to have the Maharani. She already has a large collection of budgerigars.' At the word 'budgerigar' there was a sort of snorting, squawking noise from the Maharani, and with a furious look she went and perched herself on top of the fridge, with her back to them all.

'I don't think the Maharani thinks it's

good news,' said Violet sadly. 'She doesn't look very happy about it.'

'The birds are kept in the most beautiful aviary,' Rajesh said, trying to placate the Maharani, who let out another snorting noise and refused to turn around. 'And it will be safe. No one will ever think of looking there.'

'So will all the Maharajah's money go to the government?' Johnny asked.

'Yes, it seems likely,' Rajesh sighed. 'There are still a couple of weeks left before the end of the month, but there is no reason to think that the Maharani will suddenly start talking.'

'But what will happen to the orphans?' Violet asked anxiously.

'Well,' Rajesh said, 'that is not known. But unless they can find some money from elsewhere, the orphanage will probably close and the children will be split up. Hari is very worried.'

They were all silent for a moment.

'It's a great shame that the parrot won't talk,' Johnny said.

'She's a cockatoo,' said Violet, but quietly, because she was thinking the same thing.

Rajesh had to leave shortly after. He would return the next day, he explained, to collect the Maharani and take her to Wiltshire, and he thanked them all again profusely for looking after the Maharani so kindly.

The next morning, Violet said a tearful goodbye to the Maharani before she went to school. The cockatoo regarded Violet with large, sad, accusing eyes.

'Remember, Jo,' Camille told Norma's niece, who was being left in charge of the Maharani before Rajesh came to collect her, 'you should only hand her over to a gentleman in a tweed suit called Rajesh.' Jo assured her that all would be fine.

After school, Jo picked up Violet and took her to the climbing wall and then her synchronised swimming class, so they didn't get home until it was nearly suppertime. A delighted Pudding greeted them at the door, but the house felt very empty without the Maharani.

She was just about to start her homework when the doorbell rang. Jo was busy cooking something called Pot Noodle for supper, so Violet answered the door.

It was Rajesh.

'Hello,' she said, surprised to see him. 'Is something wrong? Where's the Maharani?'

Rajesh looked puzzled. 'I am here to collect her, as we discussed. I am sorry I am a little later than I thought, but I hope that isn't a problem.'

Jo came to the door, looking concerned. 'A man came,' she said, 'at about eleven, wearing a tweed suit – like your mother said he would, Violet. The parrot didn't seem to want to go – she made a terrible racket, but I thought that was just because she liked it here . . . I'm really sorry,' she added looking very worried.

'Oh dear, that is very serious,' Rajesh said heavily.

'Angel has gone back to India, so it can't be

her this time. Do you think it's one of the criminal gangs that threatened to take her before?' Violet asked. She could feel hot tears welling up in her eyes.

'I don't know. But it isn't your fault,' Rajesh said kindly. 'It isn't anybody's fault.'

Violet nodded, knowing if she said anything she would cry.

'But where would they have taken her?' Jo asked.

Rajesh shrugged. 'Anywhere. They could have taken her absolutely anywhere.' He sighed.

Somehow the newspapers got hold of the story and over the next few days there were alleged sightings of the Maharani all over the world – but none turned out to be real. Angel made the most of the publicity, talking to the newspapers almost every day, saying what a tragedy it was and that she was doing all she could to help the police with their enquiries, but that it seemed likely to her that a criminal gang had stolen the cockatoo. She also sent Violet another very friendly postcard saying how sorry she was that the Maharani had been stolen by the criminal gang, and how nice and hot it was in India, and that she hoped Violet would have a very happy Easter.

11
THE ART OF BLUFFING

Violet was terribly upset and everyone tried to cheer her up.

A few days after the Maharani's disappearance, Dee Dee took one look at Violet's glum face and announced, 'I think I shall throw a little party. An Easter egg hunt and a tea before Rose's ballet show on Friday. Artie and I fly out to Jamaica the next day, so that will be perfect. I will telephone Lavinia and have her organise it all.'

Lavinia excelled herself. There was a

magnificent Easter egg hunt in the garden and, as it was a lovely, sunny afternoon, a delicious picnic tea was laid out with piles of hot cross buns, Easter cupcakes, chocolate crispy birds' nests, a scrumptious-looking, canary-yellow Simnel cake and, of course, piles of French Fancies. What could have been more perfect?

But, despite it all, everyone was feeling a little lacklustre.

Dee Dee was fretting about leaving Lullabelle (even though she was going to the most expensive, luxury cattery you could imagine, where each cat had their own butler), whether she had packed the right clothes and whether they would get to the airport on time.

Rose was understandably very nervous about her show and was even more quiet than usual.

And Violet? Well, she was still feeling upset about the Maharani, but she tried to make an effort to please Dee Dee.

The high point was when Art shyly presented the girls with a present each, 'because you've been so kind about school and everything,' he explained.

So, rather than dwelling on the rather

un-partyish party, let us move on to what happened next - which was that PC Green turned up, delivering an Easter egg to Dee Dee.

'Hello, Violet, Rose - any news on the parrot? We're busy following up that lead Angel gave us.'

Violet shook her head sadly.

And then, Rose's mother arrived in the most terrible fluster. Her car wouldn't start and she didn't know how they would get to the show on time. The colour drained from Rose's face.

'An emergency!' PC Green exclaimed, obviously delighted. 'Never fear, Rose, I have the squad car. We'll put on all the sirens and get you there in just a jiffy.'

'What a wonderful idea. You take the children,' Dee Dee instructed. 'Rose's mother and I will follow in a taxi as soon as we can get one.'

Outside, PC Green stood on the pavement for a moment, staring up and down the street. He had a knack of losing his car.

'Look, you've parked it there,' Violet said, pointing just across the street.

'Oh, yes, silly me,' PC Green sighed and they all got in the car. 'Sirens and lights on! Buckle up! You're in for a bumpy ride, folks!' he said, because he thought it sounded like

something a policeman might say in a film.

Nee-nah! Nee-nah! blared the sirens as they weaved through the traffic towards the West End of London where the theatre was. *Nee-nah! Nee-nah!*

Violet stared out of the window absent-mindedly. They were speeding their way down one of the backstreets near the theatre when they passed the magnificent entrance of Hardy's, the grandest hotel in London. Violet saw a familiar figure in a fur coat.

'Stop!' Violet cried, and the others looked at her in amazement.

'Why?' the three of them chorused.

'I just saw Angel, going into Hardy's.

She told us all she was going back to India,
didn't she?' Rose and Art nodded. 'And she
just sent me a postcard. What's she doing
back in England?'

'That is strange, I agree,' said PC Green.
'She has been incredibly helpful to us though,
pointing us in the direction of the criminal
gang who might have the Maharani.'

'Why would Angel pretend to be in India but really be here?' Rose asked.

'And why is she being so helpful to the police?' Art wondered.

'I guess she's changed. People do,' PC Green said, pensively.

'But perhaps she hasn't,' Art continued. 'Maybe she hasn't changed and just wants us to think she has. Perhaps she's just—'

'Bluffing!' Violet roared, interrupting Art. 'Like Johnny has been teaching me to do in poker. What if she's just been pretending to have bad cards, when she's got great ones?'

'Exactly,' Art said.

PC Green was looking mystified.

'Sorry, you've lost me. And aren't you too young to know about poker? In fact, I'm not sure that it's legal for you to know about gambling . . .'

'Let's not worry about that now,' Violet said hastily. 'PC Green, what we are all trying to say is that we think that Angel has got the

Maharani. That's why she's been pretending so hard that she hasn't.'

'Oooohhhhhh.' PC Green nodded thoughtfully. 'That would be very clever indeed. Rose, how are we doing for time?'

'I'm supposed to be at the theatre in five minutes and I really really have to be there in ten minutes,' Rose replied.

'Okey-dokey. Well, since the theatre is just round the corner, I think there is time for a very quick investigate.' And he slammed on the brakes and reversed at high speed into the forecourt in front of the entrance.

They all jumped out of the car and, ignoring the doorman who tried to descend on them, they rushed up the front stairs and into the marble lobby. They dashed past the towering Easter egg display to the main desk.

'Excuse me, my good man,' - PC Green addressed the most senior-looking concierge behind the desk, flashing his police badge. 'Do you by any chance have a lady staying here with a parrot - I mean, a cockatoo?'

The concierge's name was Derek. He silently regarded PC Green over the top of his half-moon spectacles for a long moment before replying, 'I'm sorry, sir, I'm afraid I am not at liberty to answer that question. You must understand that our guests' privacy is everything.'

'I don't think you can have looked at my badge properly. I am a policeman,' PC Green replied pompously.

'Yes, I did realise. And from your uniform, I see you are rather a junior one. I don't happen to have a badge, but I can tell you that I am the chief concierge of this establishment. It is probably the finest hotel in the whole world and we pride ourselves on our ability to protect our guests' privacy. And keeping a cockatoo in a bedroom is not, as far as I'm aware, a criminal matter. So I would kindly ask you and your friends to leave if you have no further business here.'

'It *is* a criminal matter if the bird is stolen,' PC Green pointed out curtly.

'Do you have a search warrant for this bird?'

'No,' PC Green admitted.

'Well, I suggest you return with one and then we can discuss the matter further. So until then, good day – and may I wish you all a very happy Easter. Roger the doorman will show you out.'

'Bother!' exclaimed Violet, as they stood in huddle on the pavement. 'What shall we do now?'

Before anyone could answer, PC Green's radio started talking to him, and he went off to have a conversation with it.

Rose was looking very worried indeed. 'I know it's really important to find the Maharani but I really have to go to the theatre now or I'll miss the performance,' she said. 'Sorry,' she added.

'Don't worry,' said Art. 'That's a great excuse to get rid of him.' Art gestured towards PC Green.

Violet and Rose looked at Art quizzically.

'Don't get me wrong, he's nice. But he

isn't going to be any help getting back the Maharani – it'll take him days to get a search warrant. We need to sort it out ourselves.'

The girls nodded in agreement as PC Green finished his radio conversation.

'Bad news, chaps,' he announced. 'The sergeant needs me urgently on a high-level job – something about the Lady Mayoress's cat being stuck up a tree. Bit of an emergency. So I'd better head off. I need to get that search warrant anyway – I wonder how I do that? It must be in my How to be a Police Officer manual . . .' he mused.

'Oh, PC Green,' Rose began, looking at him

pleadingly, 'please could you drop me at the theatre on the way? I'm so worried about being late.'

PC Green said, 'No problem Rose. Why don't I take all of you?'

Violet sprang into action. 'I think I'll walk actually – I feel a bit sick. I ate loads of Easter eggs,' she explained, clutching her tummy.

'Me too,' Art swiftly added, making sick noises.

PC Green looked horrified. He certainly didn't want anyone throwing up in his squad car, but then again, he wasn't quite sure he should be leaving Art and Violet on their own.

'Are you sure you'll be all right walking to the theatre?'

Both nodded at him with absolute confidence.

'I know where it is – it's just down that street and then you turn right and you're there.' Violet pointed.

'It's really near,' Art added reassuringly. 'And we'll go straight there.'

'Okey-dokey. And then I'll sort out a search warrant as soon as I find out how to get one. See you later, chaps.'

After PC Green and Rose had gone, Violet gazed up at the huge hotel. 'There must be hundreds of rooms. How will we ever find her?'

It seemed hopeless.

'Violet! Look!' Art said, pointing behind her.

Violet turned around and gasped. There was a hotel bell boy, clutching a large tin of Fortnum and Mason fruit and nut mix, walking in the main entrance.

'I don't believe it! We have to follow him!' Violet cried.

'No, wait,' said Art. 'We'll never get past reception.' Art thought hard. 'We need to create distraction or something. Or look, maybe this is a chance . . .'

An immense Mercedes drew up in front of the hotel and the doorman scurried up to it, opening doors and directing luggage to be brought out of the boot. Violet and Art's mouths dropped as an incredibly famous American actor got out of the car, along with his incredibly famous actress wife and their two children, a boy and a girl about the same age as Art and Violet.

'Follow them!' Art hissed and the pair slipped through the doors just behind the actor and his family, keeping their heads down and pretending they were part of the same group.

Once inside the lobby, they dived behind a heavily laden luggage trolley. Art poked his head above to look for the bell boy with the Fortnum and Mason tin.

'He's just getting in the lift,' Art said and the pair dashed across the busy lobby and into the lift before anyone could stop them.

'Which floor please?' asked the bell boy politely.

Violet scanned the buttons. The one for the twelfth floor was lit up.

'Floor twelve, please,' she said.

'I don't think you're right, Miss.

There are only two penthouses up there, and I don't believe you are staying in either of those.'

'Silly me, my mistake. Eleven, please,' Violet replied quickly, and he pressed the button for her.

Whoosh! The lift car sped upwards and then – *ping!* – they arrived at the eleventh floor. Art and Violet walked out nonchalantly, and then as soon as the lift doors shut behind them, they dashed for the stairs, sprinting up them two at a time.

They made it up to the next floor just in time to see the back of the bell boy disappearing down a corridor, tin held aloft.

They were about to dash after him when – *ping!* – the lift door opened again.

'Drat!' Art exclaimed, and they dived into a doorway so as not to be seen. And they were just in time, because who should appear out of the lift but the very famous actor and his family, accompanied by Derek, the grumpy concierge from the lobby.

'We are so extremely honoured that you have chosen to stay with us at Hardy's. I do hope everything is up to your absolute satisfaction, but if it's not please tell me immediately and we will do our utmost to change it. No request is too big or too small to trouble us . . .' He continued to suck up to them furiously as he opened a door along the same corridor that the bell boy had disappeared.

'The Royal Suite,' he announced with a flourish, and led the family inside.

Taking their chance, Violet and Art began to tiptoe down the corridor, but just as they did, the door to the Royal Suite began to open! Luckily, the opposite side of the corridor was lined with large windows, each draped with elaborate curtains, and the two children quickly dived behind one of them.

Derek reappeared in the corridor, still sucking up desperately. 'Of course, no problem at all, my ultimate pleasure is to serve. I will have the theatre tickets sent up immediately and then a car will call for you shortly. A light snack beforehand? The kitchens will prepare something delicious. Vintage champagne? Of course, it will be on the house. Very, very, very good, madam.' And he shut the door with a ridiculous bow.

Art and Violet listened carefully, waiting for him to call the lift and return downstairs. Then they heard another set of footsteps. It must be the bell boy, Violet decided.

'Everything okay?' Derek asked the person, who did turn out to be the bell boy.

'I suppose so. No tip though, and that parrot looks very miserable. The woman was really shouting at it when I knocked on the door.'

Violet had to stop herself from letting out a loud gasp. So Angel did have the Maharani! Violet felt fury rising up in her.

Meanwhile, the concierge and bell boy were still chatting as the two of them waited for the lift.

'I do hope the squawking doesn't trouble our extremely special guests in the Royal Suite.'

'I did tell her who was staying next door and she was very impressed.'

'Good. Maybe that will make her keep the noise down. I'll speak to her about it myself later too; I also need to have a word with her about the enormous bill she's run up.'

Ping! The lift arrived and the men's voices became fainter as the doors closed on them.

When Art and Violet were sure that the
concierge and the bell boy had gone, they
came out from behind the curtains.

'I can't believe I fell for all her bluff about
being a changed person,' Violet said to Art.

'Don't feel bad – we all believed her,' Art
said, as they looked towards the door at
the end of the corridor. They could hear the
muffled sounds of the Maharani squawking,
and Angel shouting at her. It made Violet
feel horrible.

'Art, we must hurry,' Violet urged, and they started down the hallway again.

'But how are we going to get into the room?' Art asked. 'Angel isn't just going to let you walk in and take the Maharani.'

He was right – they needed a plan! Violet looked around the corridor desperately trying to think. Then she spotted a door labelled: *Housekeeping Cupboard.*

'I've got an idea,' she announced, opening the door. Inside was a trolley, piled high with supplies and a spare maid's uniform was hanging up on the back of the door. Violet pulled on the uniform over her clothes. It nearly reached her ankles, so she tried to hoik it up using the belt. Then she pulled a cap on over her hair and picked up a pair of spectacles that were sitting on the cleaning trolley, putting those on too.

'What do you think?' Violet asked Art.

He looked doubtful. 'I think she's going to recognise you.'

'But I have to try!' Violet said, feeling irritated with Art's lack of enthusiasm. 'Have you got a better idea?'

'Perhaps, but I need to think it through.'

'There's no time,' said Violet, bossily. 'We need to save the Maharani. I'm going to try this.' And she marched down the hallway, wheeling the trolley in front of her.

She knocked on Angel's door.

'Housekeeping!' she cried in as deep a voice as she could manage, which she combined with a strange French-meets-German-with-a-bit-of-Russian accent.

The door flew open and there stood Angel, dressed in a tight, bright-pink outfit covered in sparkly stones. She looked to be in a very bad temper.

'Not now, I'm busy,' she said. Then she squinted at Violet, adding, 'I have no problem with child labour, but aren't you a little young to be a maid?'

'No, not at all, I am sixteen, just rather small for my age,' Violet replied, in her strange voice.

Angel looked at her again, more closely this time. A small smile appeared in the corner of her mouth. 'Actually, I've changed my mind. Why don't you come in and do your cleaning now?'

Excellent, Violet thought, wheeling her trolley into the room. Angel shut the door behind her. The room was a terrible mess of shopping bags, clothes and trays of half-eaten food. And in the middle of it, sitting pathetically huddled on top of a chair was the Maharani. The bird looked up to see Violet and gave a squawk of delight. Violet shook her head and looked away, hoping she would understand.

'It's okay, Violet,' said Angel, making her jump. 'You don't have to pretend you don't know the Maharani. In fact I am delighted to see you, as the wretched bird won't speak for me at all, but I'm sure you can make her talk if you really try. Time is running out and I really need that fortune.'

'How did you know . . . ?' Violet began, but then she caught sight of herself in the mirror and thought *how could Angel not have recognised me?* Art had been too polite; it was a terrible disguise.

'You know I can't make the Maharani talk,' she said to Angel. 'She hasn't spoken since the Maharajah died. She's too upset.

You might as well let us go now.'

'Let you go? Do you think I'm mad? You *will* make that bird talk, Violet, and you are not leaving this room until you do.'

Meanwhile, outside the room, Art was now stuck back behind the curtain. A steady stream of people were bringing trays of drinks and snacks, deliveries of flowers and free clothes to the film stars. Would it never end? Art wondered. He was getting worried about Violet. She and the Maharani should

have been out of there by now. What could have happened?

Finally, Art heard Derek talking to the famous actors again.

'Your car has arrived, so if you will all follow me, I will escort you to the rear entrance, where it is waiting. There are rather a large number of paparazzi at the front door, who I thought you might want to avoid.'

The actor thanked Derek, and Art heard them all leave the room, the two children squabbling away.

'Now, now, Brett Junior, Nicoletta, stop

fighting,' came the smooth, world-famous voice of their mother, as they walked towards the lift.

Ping! And then silence once again reigned in the corridor.

Art peeked out from behind the curtains and, when he was sure he was alone, he went and pressed his ear against the door to Angel's room. He could hear muffled voices, but couldn't make out what was happening. He looked through the keyhole . . . and saw a bad sight: Violet standing next to the Maharani, crying, while the bird looked miserable too.

Angel's shrill voice rang out: 'You will never see your mother and father again unless that bird talks!'

Fury and purpose filled Art as he worked out a rescue plan in his head, that (if he did say so himself) was really rather brilliant. He ran back to the film stars' door, pulling his trusty piece of wire from his pocket, and got to work.

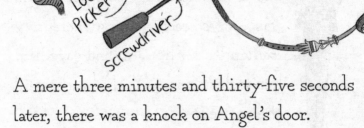

Torch

Rope

Lock Picker

Screwdriver

13
A MUCH BETTER IDEA

A mere three minutes and thirty-five seconds later, there was a knock on Angel's door.

Angel irritably opened it. In the doorway stood a very smartly dressed boy, with slicked back hair and a suit on.

'Begging your pardon, ma'am,' the boy said, in a perfect American accent, 'my name is Brett Junior Hanson. I don't know if you are aware, but my family is staying next door.'

Angel's heart gave a little leap. That was why he looked vaguely familiar to her;

she must have seen his photo in one of the celebrity magazines she was always reading. *How incredibly exciting!* she thought, and gave him her widest smile. 'Yes, I had heard,' she replied.

'Well, I am so sorry to bother you, but I have locked myself out of the room – and rather than go all the way downstairs, I wondered if I could just nip across from your roof terrace. Our terraces interconnect and I know the French doors are open on my side.'

Angel practically purred, she was so delighted to help.

'Of course! Come in, come in,' she said ushering him across the room, all the while trying to shield Violet from sight.

But the boy stopped in front of Violet and the Maharani.

'Hi, I'm Brett Junior,' he said, holding his hand out to Violet.

'Hi,' said Violet, trying not giggle. Because, as you may have realised, this wasn't Brett Junior, it was Art in disguise! And a much better disguise than Violet's costume. She shook hands with him and found he had passed her a scrap of paper. 'What a great bird!' he said, while Violet, her back to Angel, surreptitiously opened up the message.

Run as soon as we go out on the terrace. I will delay her as much as I can.

A.

'Come this way, Brett Junior. I'll show you the terrace,' gushed Angel. 'Thank you so much,' Brett Junior/Art gushed back. 'Hey, I'm guessing that with your looks you're a Bollywood movie star? My father is just Bollywood crazy at the moment. Do you think that you could introduce him to some of the right people? I'm sure he would be really grateful . . . Hey, isn't it just the most amazing view from out here? Please could you tell me what that building over there is?' he babbled whilst manoeuvring Angel so her back was to the room.

Violet wasted no time. She ran over to the door and opened it. The Maharani needed no more than a glimpse of freedom to spur her on. They both sped off into the corridor – but unfortunately Angel turned around at that moment and saw their escape.

'NO!' she cried, tottering after the pair.

'Oh, my lord, is your parrot escaping?' Art cried. 'Let me assist you in getting her back.'

Violet ran down the corridor towards the stairs, the Maharani swooping above her, dodging the light fittings. *Ping* went the lift and Derek stepped out. He looked puzzled at the sight of Violet and the Maharani dashing past him and into the stairwell.

A moment later Art and Angel appeared.

'Ah, madam,' he said. 'There is the small matter of your bill. I have it here.'

'Not now!' panted Angel. 'Besides, I won't be able to pay it unless I catch that dratted bird!'

'In that case, madam, let me help you! I suggest we take the lift and head them off. The first floor will probably be the best place.'

They all jumped in and he hit the button marked 'One'.

'I'm sorry – I'm not sure we have been introduced?' Derek said turning to Art.

Angel answered for him, girly and starstruck again. 'This is Brett Junior, from the suite next door.'

Derek looked at Art carefully. *Ping* went the lift, as it arrived at the first floor.

'I think we both know that's not true,' he said to Art. 'In fact, didn't I see you earlier in reception with the young lady who has now kidnapped the cockatoo?'

'You're right,' Art agreed, and as the doors opened he dashed out of the lift towards the stairs. Angel lunged for him but was too late. Sprinting into the stairwell, he nearly bumped straight into Violet and the squawking Maharani.

'Hurry! They're right behind us!' Art yelled, pulling her down the stairs to the next floor.

They rushed down to the ground floor and charged into the lobby, practically careering into a crowd of tourists as they made for the main doors. But alas, at that moment the concierge and Angel appeared out of the lift, blocking their route.

'Come on, this way!' Art cried, heading in the opposite direction.

They ran through some double doors and found themselves in the dining room. It was an enormous and enormously grand room, with paintings of fat goddesses all over the walls, a fountain in the middle, and leafy palm trees in vast pots. Waiters in tails walked sedately around holding silver platters aloft, and the dinner guests, all dressed up in their finest gowns and suits, spoke in hushed voices while a string quartet gently played in the corner.

As you can imagine, Violet, Art and the Maharani's arrival did not go down too well.

They slalomed between the tables and the waiters, with the Maharani ducking and swooping, accompanied by a universal spluttering from the dinner guests.

'I say, is that a parrot?'

'Isn't that against health and safety?'

'A parrot in the dining room – I never heard of such a thing!'

'Good Lord, they seem in a hurry.'

The two children and the bird headed for the large swing doors into the kitchen, both Art and Violet thinking that there must be a door to the street from there. But Derek, who had arrived in the dining room just moments after the trio, quickly signalled to the head waiter, who in turn signalled to his team of waiters. They closed ranks as efficiently as an army and zoomed in front of the children, blocking their escape.

Art and Violet frantically doubled back on themselves, but the doors by which they had entered the dining room were now blocked by Angel.

Panic rose in both their stomachs. There seemed to be no escape . . .

Then Violet spotted a door hiding behind a large palm tree. She sped towards it and the others followed. It was not until she got right up to it that she saw it was very unpromisingly labelled LADIES. Nevertheless, they all dived through it.

Hardy's was so grand that they employed

a lady to sit in the toilets and keep them spotless, and help the customers with hand towels. The lady's name was Betty, and Betty was large and friendly and liked a laugh. And laugh is what she did when she saw two children and a cockatoo pile into her toilet.

'What are you lot doing?' she giggled.

'Running away from the head concierge. We're trying to escape from the hotel,' Violet panted at her.

Now it just so happened that Betty was none too pleased with Derek. He had just refused to give her a small pay rise while awarding himself an enormous one, which she considered the height of stinginess and very unfair, as she didn't get paid much and did her job extremely well, putting up with a good deal of rudeness with a shrug and a smile. Here was her chance for a little bit of revenge. Besides, she liked the look of Violet and Art.

'I see. Well, that window over there, which happens to be open a little bit, leads straight out into the street. But you didn't hear it from me, okay! I'll hold them off for a bit.'

'Thank you so much!' Art said, as he shoved up the window and the two children clambered out, with the Maharani flapping behind them.

The door burst open again as one of the

waiters tried to come in, but Betty was ready for him.

'What do you think you are doing? You're a man! You can't come in here. I've got customers.' She stood in his way.

'But the children and the parrot?' he argued. 'I must get them.'

'What children and a parrot?' Betty played dumb. 'What are you talking about?'

Derek appeared in the doorway. 'The parrot and children who just came in here,' he said coldly. 'Let us in, Betty.'

'Okay.' Betty stood out of the way. 'But I haven't seen any children and definitely not a parrot. Maybe I did hear something, but I was so busy doing my job, cleaning the toilets.'

Derek, the waiters, the head waiter and, last of all, Angel, all piled into the small toilets. The open window stared at them.

Angel and Derek scrambled out into the dark street. It was empty. Art, Violet and the Maharani had gone.

'Oh dear, madam,' Derek sighed. 'They seem to have escaped. Please accept my sincerest apologies.'

Angel let out a long stream of very rude words.

With the Maharani perched happily on her shoulder and Art by her side, Violet headed towards the theatre, where Rose's ballet show was in full swing. The streets were busy with late-night shoppers and tourists, and the sun was setting, turning the sky a beautiful marmalade colour.

They hadn't walked far when a large, modern building loomed up ahead of them, all lit up like a spaceship. At the sight of it, the Maharani began to squawk excitedly.

'Do you know what that building is?' Violet asked Art, for she had no idea.

He shrugged and shook his head in reply.

But the Maharani seemed to know it very well and, as they walked past its glass entrance doors, she squawked even more loudly and flew off Violet's shoulder.

'Maharani!' Violet protested. 'Come back now! You can't go in there.' But the bird wasn't listening and the doors glided silently open for her.

Violet and Art ran after her, calling her name. They found themselves in a huge glass hall, entirely empty except for a desk in the centre of it. Behind the desk stood a young woman, immaculate in a red dress, with large spectacles and very tidy blonde hair. She reminded Violet a little of Lavinia, Dee Dee's organiser. The young woman raised her arm and the Maharani gently landed on it.

'Good evening, your Royal Highness,' the lady greeted the Maharani. 'And may I wish you a happy Easter. We have been waiting for you to come and visit us. Just in time I see, by the date. May I offer you or your guests some refreshment before we begin?'

The bird nodded appreciatively and the lady produced a tin of Fortnum and Mason fruit and nut mix from her desk and emptied a little into a bowl for the Maharani, who hopped off her arm and started to gobble it down. The young lady walked over to Art and Violet, who were still standing by the door, looking completely confused.

'Good evening, please come in. You are most welcome as guests of Her Majesty's. May I introduce myself? I am Rebecca, and I will be here to assist the Maharani through the first part of the proceedings. May I get you something to drink? A hot chocolate perhaps?'

They both nodded, too surprised to speak. Rebecca walked off and reappeared peculiarly quickly with two cups of frothy, steaming hot chocolate with whipped cream and flakes stuck in the top.

'I'm so sorry,' Rebecca said, 'but I didn't catch your names.'

'Art and Violet. Violet has been looking after the Maharani,' Art replied. 'I'm sorry, but we're a little confused. Would you mind telling me where we are?'

Rebecca smiled. 'Of course. This is the international headquarters of the Lucre bank. We manage all of the Maharajah's affairs – and the Maharani is here, I imagine, about the Maharajah's will.'

Art and Violet's mouths dropped. But there was little time to think, only to gulp down their hot chocolate, as Rebecca led them off.

'The bank looks after the Maharajah's

fortune,' she explained. 'But it's divided into different parts: stocks and shares, gold bullion, jewels, and of course his properties, which are not actually kept in the bank, obviously – but the ownership papers are. According to the Maharajah's will, the Maharani is now in charge of all these things, so we'll have to visit each department and they will release each part to the Maharani – if and only if, she can provide the necessary passwords.'

Violet's heart sank. 'She hasn't spoken since the Maharajah died,' she said. 'Not a word.'

Rebecca looked concerned. 'Well, since you are here, let us try.'

Rebecca led them up a glass spiral staircase

and into a lobby, dimly lit by a large roof light. Its walls were lined with identical doors.

'Stocks and shares first,' Rebecca explained, opening one of the doors.

Art and Violet couldn't believe the noise. Banks of television screens blared out business news to row upon row of men and women sitting in front of computer screens, shouting into telephones.

'The markets are closing in New York soon,' Rebecca explained. 'Things always get a little tense.'

A man in a pinstripe suit and bright red tie got up from a desk.

'Ah, here comes Crispin,' Rebecca replied.

'Majesty,' Crispin greeted the Maharani, and nodded at Art and Violet. They all stood awkwardly for a moment, waiting for the Maharani to speak. Quite a long moment.

'The password if you please, Your Most Excellent Highness,' Crispin prompted.

There was another long silence while the Maharani stared into space.

'Um, I don't think this is going to work,' Art said.

'Maybe I should just take her home,' Violet agreed.

But then, just as they were about to turn and go, the Maharani suddenly said: *'To be or not to be? That is the question.'*

Violet and Art looked at the cockatoo in amazement.

'Excellent. Like the Maharajah, I do love Shakespeare,' said Crispin and handed a bundle of papers to Rebecca.

'Well done, Your Majesty!' Rebecca said and led them back into the silent lobby.

'I think we'll go to jewellery next,' Rebecca announced, opening another door.

They walked into a tiny, octagonal room with a very high ceiling and shimmering gold walls. A small elderly lady, with large green glasses and bright pink hair, draped in soft velvets and clunky beads, sat behind a small desk.

She came forward, greeting the Maharani

respectfully and shaking Violet and Art's hands.

'I am Magenta Lowder,' she introduced herself. 'Now, Your Majesty, what do you want to say to me?'

This time the Maharani barely hesitated: '*All that glisters is not gold.*'

'Well done!' grinned Magenta and she fetched a red box on wheels with a handle, a bit like a suitcase, that Rebecca could pull along behind her.

'Property next,' Rebecca announced when they were back in the lobby.

Another door opened, revealing what can only be described as the living room of a large country house. A Labrador leaped off

a chintzy sofa and came bounding towards them, ignoring the Maharani's withering looks. A gentleman wearing tweed breeches and smoking a pipe got up from behind a desk. 'What ho!' he greeted them, in the poshest of accents. 'Now, Your Royal Maj, are you going to do your stuff?'

The Maharani obviously thought this wasn't quite respectful enough and gave him a disdainful look. But then she did go on to say: '*Better a witty fool than a foolish wit.*'

'Jolly good show,' the gentleman replied and handed over a crisp white envelope.

'Last and not least,' Rebecca said as they walked back to the lobby, 'the gold bullion.'

And she opened another door.

Violet and Art felt as if they were walking into a church vault. A man, dressed all in black, with a vicar-like air came towards them, his hands held behind his back.

'Oh, Maharani, Your Majesty, what a pleasure to see you again! How are you coping with your terrible loss?'

The Maharani seemed to shrink down into herself and her feathers drooped.

'I'm so sorry, I didn't mean to upset you, Your Highness. Time is the greatest of healers. Now, do you have anything you want to say to me?'

The Maharani gave a little shudder and sat

with her head on her chest and said nothing. 'There is no hurry,' the man said again. 'Whenever you are ready.'

The Maharani buried her head further.

Rebecca exchanged looks with Art and Violet. Violet stroked the Maharani gently, and she was rewarded with the cockatoo poking out one eye.

'Can you remember the password?' Violet asked gently.

The bird nodded.

'Will you say it, just for me? Then we are nearly finished and we can go home.'

The cockatoo raised its head and shook itself. '*Death is a fearful thing*,' she said in a clear voice, before collapsing back into Violet's neck.

Everyone made sympathetic noises to the poor Maharani.

The vicarish man went over to the stone table that served as his desk. He pressed a button and the floor opened. A small platform lift came up with twenty large gold bars on it, on a small trolley. Rebecca briskly picked up the pulley handle and wheeled it, along with the jewellery case, back into the lobby.

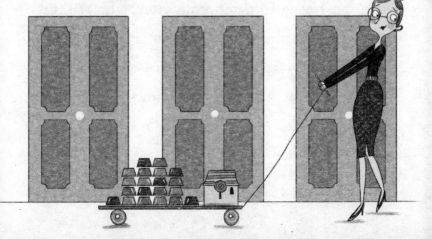

A lady with short grey hair, bright red lipstick and wearing a smart grey suit was waiting for them. She greeted the Maharani and then introduced herself to Violet and Art as Grace Crimble, Head of Lucre's, and thanked them for escorting the Maharani to the bank.

'Well, Maharani, congratulations, you have retrieved all the Maharajah's treasures – and just in time too. A few hours later and the fortune would have gone to the government. You now need to name your heir, who will be free to distribute the money, art, jewellery, and property as they see fit, or alternatively keep it for themselves. Now, Maharani, the Maharajah had many learned and wise friends – have you thought carefully about who to choose?'

The Maharani nodded.

'Very good. Please tell me of your decision.'

The Maharani, ever the actress, paused theatrically for effect. And then she announced in a clear voice, '*Violet. Violet Remy-Robinson.*'

And everyone, including Violet, gasped.

BOCHIR TIMES

29th May

The Opening of the New Palace Museum

Today is a very special day for the residents of Bochir. A new, magnificent museum will open in the Maharajah's old palace in the city to display his fantastic art and jewellery collection.

The museum will be opened by Miss Violet Remy-Robinson of London, whom readers will remember was named the Maharajah's heir by his cockatoo, known as the Maharani. The citizens of this city owe Miss Remy-Robinson a considerable debt, as she kept nothing of the Maharajah's fortune for herself. Instead, all the money went towards helping the orphans of the city, funding the new hospital, a tiger sanctuary and, of course, the museum.

The opening ceremony will be at four o'clock this afternoon and Miss Remy-Robinson will of course be accompanied by the Maharani, who now lives with The Remy-Robinsons in London.

MUMBAI REPORTER

REVIEW OF *LOVE IS LOVELY* – NIL STARS OUT OF FIVE

0/5

Last night saw the lavish opening of *Love is Lovely*, one of the most expensive films ever made in Bollywood and entirely funded by its star, the hitherto unknown actress, Angel. But unfortunately not even the stunning costumes and spectacular dance scenes can save this movie from being an absolute disaster from beginning to end, mostly because of Miss Angel's very poor performance. To say she is wooden would be an insult to trees. I do feel sympathy for the poor lady, as apparently she has spent every last penny she has on the film, but I can only urge my readers to avoid it at all costs.

27th December

Review of *The Nutcracker* by the Youth Ballet, and *Charlie and the Chocolate Factory* by the Wright School for the Performing Arts.

What a bumper year it has been for children's dramatic arts! Following the Youth Ballet's storming production of *Sleeping Beauty* at Easter, the company's young prima ballerina, Rose Trelawney, triumphs again in the lead role of Clara, in *The Nutcracker* well supported by a number of other talented young dancers.

I then crossed town to watch the prestigious Wright School's Christmas production of *Charlie and the Chocolate Factory*. All the main characters were excellent, as I have come to expect from London's finest stage school, but the star of the show was undoubtedly new pupil Arthur 'Art' Brown, who played Charlie. He quite simply stole the show.

We look forward to seeing much more of Art in the future!

Weather forecast: Rain.

14th January

Birdhouse Extension Wins Small Projects Competition

We are pleased to announce that the winner of our annual small projects competition is Mr Benedict Remy-Robinson of RR Architects for his small extension to his flat to house his daughter's pet cockatoo. The exquisitely designed structure resembles a mini Indian palace, but with underfloor heating and an elaborate perch for the bird. Mr Remy-Robinson said how delighted he was to have received the prize. He also

admitted that he hadn't been best pleased when the cockatoo first came to live with his family, but that now he couldn't imagine life without her.

Violet's extra-helpful word glossary

Violet loves words, especially if they sound unusual, so some of the words used in her story might have been a little tricky to understand. Most of them you probably know, but Violet has picked out a few to explain . . .

Maharajah – A Maharajah is an Indian Prince. And by the way, Bochir is a made-up place.

Benefactor – This is a very kind and generous person who supports a project with money and often advice too.

Dhal and Samosas – Types of yummy Indian food.

Shakespeare – He was a very famous English writer who wrote plays, for example *Romeo and Juliet*.

Gnarled – I think this is a great word! It means something that's twisted and knobbly.

Pliés – Rose had to explain this to me, because I know nothing about ballet. This is one of the first moves you learn as a ballet dancer.

Being detained at his Majesty's pleasure – Dee Dee had to explain this to me. But it's a polite way of saying someone is in prison.

Fortnum and Mason – A very grand shop in London, that is famous for its fancy food. The Maharani is lucky to have food delivered from there!

Bollywood – The Indian version of Hollywood. It is in Mumbai which is the biggest city in India.

Reclusive – This means that you hide away because you don't like seeing other people.

Con-artist – A person who cheats or tricks people, usually into giving him or her lots of money.

Detention – You're lucky if you don't know what this is. A detention is a punishment at school where you either have to stay behind at break-time or after school.

Mon Dieu – My mother says this sometimes and I tell her off. It means 'My God' in French.

Kuala Lumpur – The capital of Malaysia.

Traumatised – This means that you are very upset by something that has happened to you.

Texas Hold 'Em – Isn't this just the best name for a game? It makes me think of cowboys and the Wild West, but really it's a type of poker game (although if my mother asks, of course I don't know that...)

Tuxedo – A smart black jacket that men (and women sometimes) wear with a bow tie for a party or a wedding.

Mannequin heads – These are those rather creepy doll-like heads that you keep wigs on.

Aviary – A special house for birds.

Lacklustre – this means a bit dull and not much fun.

Concierge and bell boy – These are both jobs in a hotel. A concierge is usually works behind the front desk and the bell boy carries luggage or runs errands for people.

Stocks and Shares – My dad says these are little bits of a big company that you can buy and that can earn you money (or lose it!).

Gold bullion – Big bars of gold. The ones in the bank were very shiny.

Have you solved all the Violet mysteries?